ARCHER ARMADILLO'S SECRET ROOM

by Marilyn Singer
Pictures by Beth Lee Weiner

Macmillan Publishing Company
New York

Collier Macmillan Publishers
London

Macmillan Publishing Company
866 Third Avenue, New York, N.Y. 10022
Collier Macmillan Canada, Inc.
Printed in the United States of America
10 9 8 7 6 5 4 3 2 1

Library of Congress Cataloging in Publication Data
Singer, Marilyn.
Archer Armadillo's secret room.
Summary: Archer Armadillo refuses to leave his secret
room when the rest of his family moves to a new burrow.
1. Children's stories, American. [1. Armadillos—
Fiction. 2. Moving, Household—Fiction] I. Weiner,
Beth Lee, ill. II. Title.
PZ7.S6172Ar   1985   [E]   84-20087
ISBN 0-02-782700-3

To Asher
—M. S.

To Meredith, with love
—B. L.W.

Archer Armadillo figured his burrow was the best burrow in the whole state of Texas. It was warm. It was snug. And it had lots of rooms Archer could explore.

His grandfather—whom everyone, even Archer, called Old Paw—agreed with him. After all, the burrow had been Old Paw's before Archer and his mother and his father and his twelve brothers all moved into it. Old Paw had lived there since he was small.

Sometimes, after Archer went exploring the burrow, he'd tell his grandfather what he found. And Old Paw would laugh or look surprised or scratch his belly.

Once, in one of the rooms, Archer found an empty shell of armor just like his own, only bigger and harder and dustier. When he told Old Paw, his grandfather slapped the ground and said, "Why, that must be my great-uncle Manus. We always wondered what happened to him."

Another time, Archer found a whole room full of
roots. He stuffed himself and couldn't even eat his
weevils at dinner. His mother scolded him but his
grandfather said, "My, I'm hungry tonight. I do
believe I'll eat all the leftovers." And he winked at
Archer.

But there was one room that Archer never told Old Paw about. It was the room Archer liked best of all. It was tiny and narrow and it smelled a little musty. But there Archer could curl up and snooze or fight off coyotes or be a giant prehistoric armadillo like his great-great-great-great-great-etc.-great-grandfather Dasypus, who was twelve feet long.

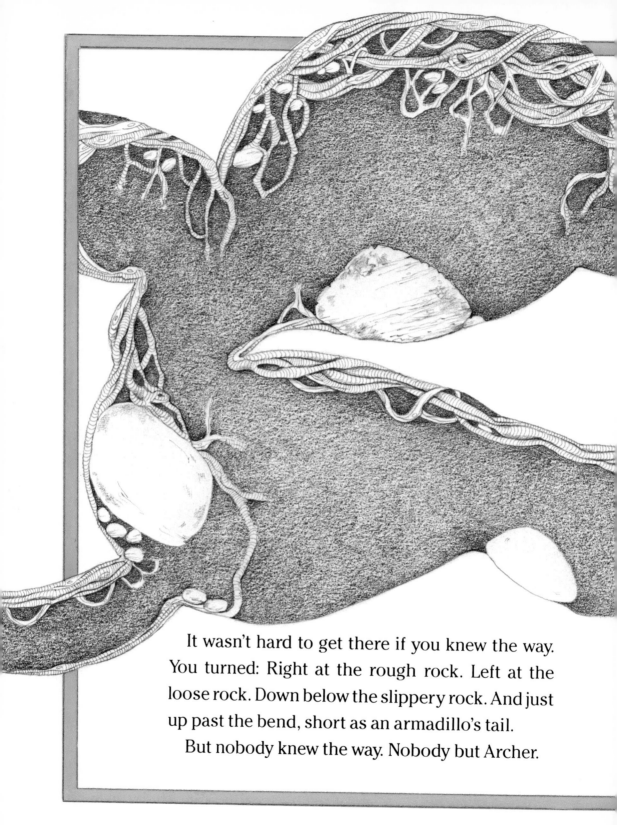

It wasn't hard to get there if you knew the way. You turned: Right at the rough rock. Left at the loose rock. Down below the slippery rock. And just up past the bend, short as an armadillo's tail.

But nobody knew the way. Nobody but Archer.

Then, one evening when the Armadillo family was admiring the setting sun reflected in the little pool by their burrow, Archer's father announced that he had a surprise for everyone.

"Mosquitos!" one of Archer's brothers exclaimed.

"Swimming lessons!" said another.

"A trip to Brazil?" asked Archer, thinking of his big cousins, Pedro and Anita, who lived there.

"No," said Archer's father. "It's better than any of those. It's a new burrow."

"A new burrow!" said Archer's mother. "How exciting!"

"A new burrow!" yelled Archer's brothers. "Yippee!"

"Hmmm," said Old Paw, scratching his belly.

But Archer didn't say a word.

"Let's go look at it," said Archer's father.
Everyone agreed.

Except Archer. He looked at his grandfather. "I'd rather stay here," he said. "Wouldn't you, Old Paw?"

"Nonsense!" his father exclaimed. "Our water hole is drying up and we need a new place to live."

"Hmmm," said Old Paw again. "I think I will have a look at this new burrow."

"That's the spirit, Old Paw," said Archer's father. And he and Archer's mother and Archer's twelve brothers, each trying to be first in line, trooped off merrily. Old Paw followed, murmuring "Hmmm" to himself every once in a while. And Archer trailed way behind, dragging his feet and drooping his head.

When they arrived, Archer's brothers ran inside and out, whooping and hollering. Old Paw walked around slowly, poking at the walls, sniffing at the floor. But Archer stayed outside and stared at the ground.

Finally, everyone came back out. Archer's father said, "It's very old and it needs a little work, but I've always been good with my claws."

"Do *you* like it, Archer?" asked his mother.

"No!" Archer shouted. And he rushed into a bush and rolled up tightly into a ball.

The next day, the Armadillos rustled and bustled and moved into their new burrow.

"Isn't it wonderful?" everyone said.

Everyone but Old Paw and Archer. Old Paw didn't say much, so no one knew what he was thinking. But Archer tried to tell everyone else that he thought the new burrow was awful. He hated the smell and the shape and the fresh twigs decorating his new room. He missed his soft, leafy bed. He missed his store of berries. He missed his secret room. But no one wanted to listen to him.

I'm not going to stay here, he decided. So that afternoon, while everyone slept, he sneaked out, raced for his old home and hurried inside.

He turned right at the rough rock. He turned left at the loose rock. He slid down below the slippery rock and just up past the bend, short as an armadillo's tail. And then he was sitting in his secret room. "They'll never find me now," he said out loud. "Never. Ever." He chuckled to himself and happily munched some berries. Then he snuggled against a wall and slept.

When Archer woke up, he was hungry. "Is dinner ready?" he called. But then he remembered that there was no one around to get him his dinner.

I could try scratching for ants, he thought, but my claws aren't strong enough and my tongue isn't long enough yet. Archer sighed and ate some more berries. He was still hungry.

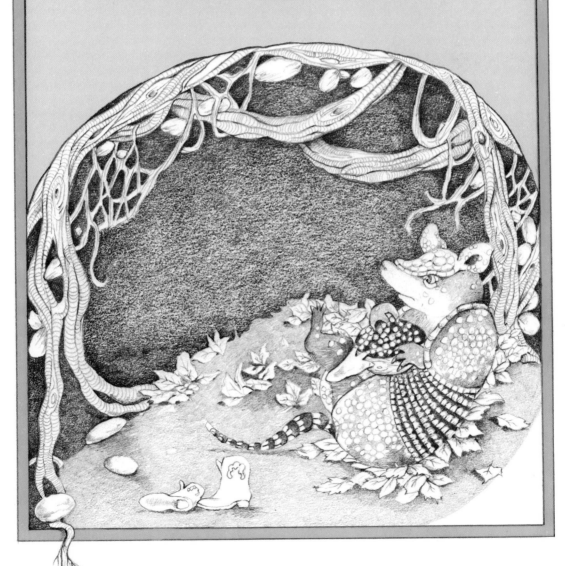

"Never mind," he reassured himself. "I'm back in my secret room in the best burrow in Texas and nobody can make me go."

But this time, he didn't feel quite so happy.

He tried pretending to fight some coyotes, but after a while he became bored. "I guess I'll take another nap," he said.

And he curled up and closed his eyes. But he couldn't fall asleep at all. Soon he got up and began to pace the floor.

"This room is much smaller than it used to be," he said. He scrabbled out and peered about.

This burrow is darker and colder than it used to be, thought Archer. And it smells empty. I wonder if anyone misses me.

Just then Archer heard a noise coming down the tunnel. A pattering, skittering noise like paws on pebbles. He heard the noise turn right at the rough rock. He heard it turn left at the loose rock. He heard it clatter down below the slippery rock. And when it got to the bend, short as an armadillo's tail, Archer rushed back into his room.

"Who's that?" he tried to say. But the words wouldn't come out.

The sound slid one step closer.

Archer shivered, stepped backward and fell with a bump over a root he forgot was there. "Ow," he whimpered.

And then, in the doorway, he saw two eyes glittering above a shadowy, pointed snout.

"Aa-ee!" Archer squealed and tried frantically to dig a hole in the floor of his room.

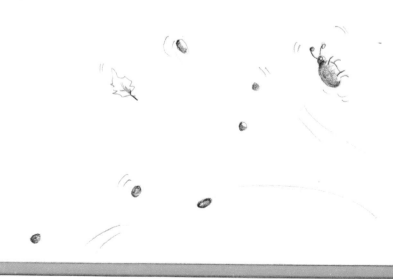

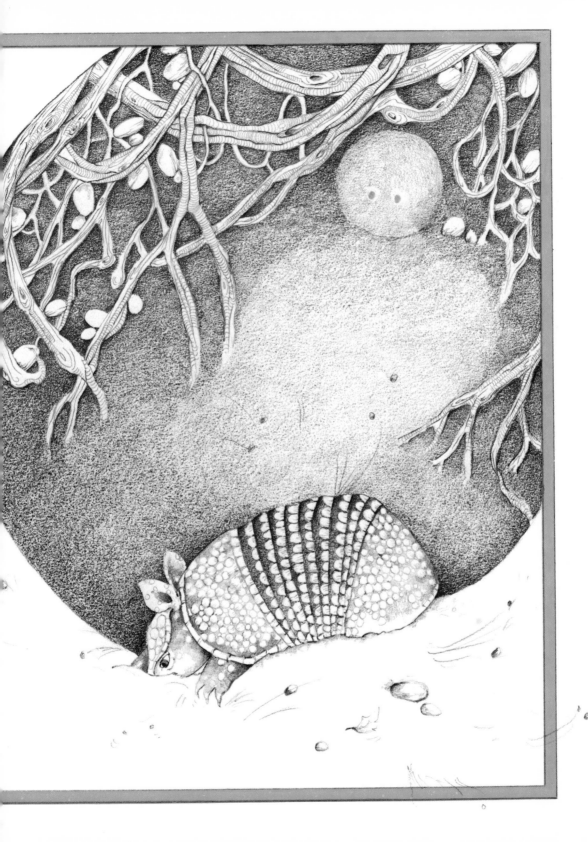

"Who's that?" rasped a familiar voice. "What's going on?"

Archer abruptly stopped digging. "Old Paw! Is that you?"

"It's me, all right," answered his grandfather, stepping into the room.

"What are you doing here?" asked Archer.

"The same thing you're doing. I'm running away," said Old Paw.

"You can't run away."

"Why not?"

"Because—because you're—you're too old!" Archer said.

"Says who?" said Old Paw. "I love this old burrow. Here I was born and here I'm going to stay." He shook out some leaves, arranged them in a neat pile, lay down on them and closed his eyes.

Archer didn't know what to do. He nudged his grandfather. "But Old Paw, if you stay here, who's going to get weevils and ants and roots for you to eat?"

Old Paw opened his eyes a little. "I will. I may be a little stiff and a little slow, but I'll manage." He shut his eyes again and rolled away from Archer.

Archer trotted around to Old Paw's other side
and nudged him even harder. "But Old Paw, if you
stay here, you'll have to clean this whole burrow all
by yourself!"

This time, Old Paw didn't bother to open his
eyes. "I'll only clean the rooms I use. And *you* can
help me," he said in a sleepy voice. Then he let out
a huge snore.

Archer got upset. He didn't know what to say. He thought and thought. Then he nudged Old Paw very hard indeed. "But Old Paw, if you stay here, Mom and Dad and Angus, Austin, Arthur, Amos, Alistair, Alfred, Andrew, Albert, Arnold, Ambrose, Asher and Abie will all miss you."

Slowly, Old Paw opened his eyes. "Hmmm," he said. "You think so?"

"Yes. They probably miss you right now."

"Hmmm. Well. Well," Old Paw said.

Then he was quiet for so long that Archer finally blurted out, "Old Paw, if you go to live in the new burrow, I will, too."

"You will?" said Old Paw, raising his head and looking right at Archer.

Archer swallowed hard. "I will," he said, nodding his head.

"Well, in that case, it's a deal!" said Old Paw.

"But before we go," Archer said, in a small, sad voice, "could we say good-by to our old home?"

"That's a right fine idea," agreed Old Paw.

Together they walked through the burrow.

They said good-by to the room full of roots.

They said good-by to great-uncle Manus (or what was left of him).

They said good-by to all the rooms they'd never explore.

At last, they went back to the secret room. Archer touched the walls gently. "Adios," he whispered.

Then, suddenly, he turned to his grandfather. "Old Paw, how did you find this room? It was my secret room."

Old Paw chuckled. "It was my secret room, too, when I was a little armadillo."

"Do you think there'll be a secret room in the new burrow?"

"Oh, I'll bet there is. If you explore well, you'll find it."

"I will. I'll explore very well. And when I find it, I'll let you use it, too. Sometimes."

Then he and Old Paw smiled at each other.

And they went down the bend, short
as an armadillo's tail, up above the
slippery rock, right at the loose
rock, left at the rough rock, out
of the burrow and down the road
together to their new home.